Contents

THE TEEN AND THE VANISHING TOWN

UNREVEALING THE DISAPPEARANCE

AYESHA ASHFAQUE

Made with ♥ on the Notion Press Platform
www.notionpress.com

Foreword

The Teen and the Vanishing Town is a captivating journey into the unknown, where secrets hide beneath the surface and nothing is as it seems. In this thrilling tale, Ayesha Ashfaque weaves a story that grips the reader from the very first page. With a keen sense of suspense, mystery, and adventure, she invites us into a world where a young teen unravels the truth behind a town on the brink of disappearing.

Through the eyes of her protagonist, Ayesha explores themes of curiosity, bravery, and the pursuit of truth, while crafting an atmosphere of intrigue and uncertainty. Readers will find themselves drawn into the mystery, eager to solve the puzzle along with the characters. This book is a testament to Ayesha's storytelling prowess, where every twist and turn leaves an indelible mark. Prepare for an unforgettable adventure in a town that refuses to stay hidden.

Preface

The Teen and the Vanishing Town is a story born from my fascination with mysteries and the unknown. As a young writer, I've always been drawn to tales that keep readers on the edge of their seats, where every twist and turn brings them closer to an unexpected revelation. This book is my attempt to capture that essence of suspense, adventure, and the thrill of discovery.

In this story, I wanted to explore how one person's curiosity and determination can uncover secrets that have been hidden for years. The journey of a teenager uncovering the truth in a town that seems to be fading away reflects my own belief that sometimes, the most important answers lie in the places we least expect.

I hope that as you read The Teen and the Vanishing Town, you are taken on a journey filled with excitement and mystery, where every page brings you closer to the truth. Thank you for joining me in this adventure. I hope you enjoy it as much as I enjoyed writing it.

Acknowledgements

I would like to express my heartfelt gratitude to everyone who has been a part of this journey. First and foremost, I am deeply thankful to my family for their constant support, encouragement, and belief in my writing. Without their love and understanding, this book would not have been possible.

A special thank you to my friends, whose ideas, feedback, and enthusiasm helped shape this story. Their encouragement motivated me to push through challenges and keep writing.

I would also like to acknowledge the teachers, mentors, and all those who have inspired me along the way. Their guidance has been invaluable in shaping my passion for storytelling.

Finally, to the readers—thank you for picking up this book and joining me on this adventure. Your support means the world to me. This book is for all of you who dare to believe in the mysteries of the unknown.

Prologue

The night Hollowbrook vanished, it wasn't like anything you'd expect from a typical small-town disappearance. No dramatic explosions, no loud crashes. It wasn't even sudden—at least, not in the way you think. One moment, the town was alive. People were laughing, lights flickered in windows, and the streets hummed with the rhythm of daily life. But by dawn, it was as if Hollowbrook had never existed at all.

When I stepped outside that morning, I was met with a chilling emptiness. There were no cars, no distant chatter, no footsteps echoing on the pavement. Not a single soul remained. The fog wrapped around the town like a suffocating blanket, hiding what remained beneath. The wind carried a whisper, though no one was there to speak it. I could feel it in the air—the town's heartbeat had stopped.

I wasn't sure what was happening, but I knew one thing for certain: I couldn't just stand there and wait for answers to appear. I had to find out what had happened to Hollowbrook—and why I was the only one left to see it.

ONE

A Town Like No Other

Hollowbrook wasn't the kind of town that appeared on postcards, and if you asked the locals, most would probably describe it as "charming" or "quaint." But beneath the small-town facade, there was something... different. Something that whispered in the wind and lingered in the shadows. To an outsider, it might seem normal—just another sleepy town tucked away between the hills. But to those of us who had lived here long enough, Hollowbrook had a way of getting under your skin.

It had always been that way.

I had grown up in Hollowbrook, and over the years, I'd gotten used to the strange little things that made it unique. The way the air always smelled like fresh pine, the old cobblestone streets that seemed to shift slightly with each season, and the way time felt like it moved a little slower here than anywhere else. Maybe that's what made the town feel so... timeless. Or maybe it was the fact that no matter how many times you tried to leave, it always had a way of pulling you back in.

I lived on the edge of town, on a street lined with crooked houses that seemed like they had stories of their own to tell. The one I lived in wasn't much different. A two-story place with peeling shutters and ivy creeping up the side, it looked like it belonged in one of those old black-and-white photos you find tucked away in a dusty attic.

It was late afternoon when everything started to change. I was sitting on the front steps, like I usually did after school, when I noticed it—a strange quiet had fallen over the town. No children running down the street. No dogs barking. Even the birds seemed to have stopped singing. It was an eerie stillness, one I couldn't shake off.

I had always been good at noticing things, small details that others overlooked. And today, those details were telling me that something was wrong.

At first, I thought it might just be the weather—Hollowbrook was known for its strange storms, the kind that rolled in without warning. But there was no storm. Just the unsettling silence.

Then, out of the corner of my eye, I saw something even stranger. A figure standing near the edge of the woods, just outside town. It was too far away to make out any details, but the figure was still. As if it had been waiting for something.

I didn't know it at the time, but that figure was the first sign of the mystery that would soon consume Hollowbrook. Something was about to happen, something I couldn't yet understand.

But I felt it in my gut, that familiar, sinking feeling that told me this wasn't going to be one of those typical days. It wasn't going to be just another quiet afternoon in a town that always seemed stuck in time.

This time, Hollowbrook wasn't just strange—it was about to disappear.

TWO

THE VANISHING ACT

I didn't sleep well that night. The strange figure at the edge of the woods and the unnatural stillness of the town gnawed at my mind, refusing to let go. I kept replaying the scene in my head, trying to convince myself that it was nothing—just a trick of the light or my imagination running wild. But deep down, I knew better.

When morning came, the sun was hidden behind a thick layer of clouds, casting a pale, gray light over Hollowbrook. It was the kind of morning that made the whole town feel like it was holding its breath, waiting for something to happen. I shook off the uneasy feeling as best as I could and got ready for school.

Ben was waiting for me at the corner, just like he always did. We'd been friends since we were kids, bonded by our shared curiosity about the town's oddities. He was the only person I knew who shared my sense that Hollowbrook wasn't as ordinary as it seemed.

"Did you feel it yesterday?" I asked as we walked toward school.

"Feel what?" Ben replied, adjusting the straps of his worn-out backpack.

"The quiet. The way the town just... stopped."

Ben glanced at me, his brow furrowing. "Yeah, now that you mention it. It was weird. Like everything was frozen for a moment."

I nodded. "And there was someone standing by the woods. Just standing there, watching."

Ben's eyes widened a bit. "Did you see who it was?"

I shook my head. "Too far away."

We walked in silence for a few minutes, the sound of our footsteps on the pavement the only noise around us. Even the usual morning bustle of the town felt subdued.

When we arrived at school, the strange feeling didn't go away. In fact, it intensified. The halls were quieter than usual, and there was an air of tension that seemed to hang over everything. Our classmates whispered to each other, casting nervous glances out the windows. Something was definitely wrong.

In homeroom, Mrs. Holloway, our usually chipper teacher, looked pale and distracted. She kept glancing at her phone, her hands shaking slightly as she tried to maintain her composure. It wasn't long before we found out why.

At the start of the first period, the principal's voice crackled over the intercom.

"Students, please remain in your classrooms until further notice. We are experiencing some... unexpected issues this morning."

The announcement only made the tension worse. Everyone began to murmur, exchanging worried looks. Unexpected issues? That wasn't something we heard every day.

Ben leaned over to me. "What do you think's going on?"

I shrugged, but my mind was racing. Whatever was happening, it wasn't normal.

The morning dragged on, each minute feeling like an hour. Teachers tried to keep up with their lessons, but it was clear their minds were elsewhere. The atmosphere in the school was suffocating, the silence in the hallways almost deafening. By lunchtime, the rumors were spreading like wildfire.

"Did you hear? People are saying a bunch of houses are empty this morning."

"Yeah, like the whole Jenkins family just... vanished."

"And the Thompsons, too."

The more I heard, the more my unease grew. Families disappearing overnight? It couldn't be true. But deep down, I knew there was something to it. Something big was happening in Hollowbrook, and it was more than just a few families missing.

Ben and I decided to skip the rest of the day. We needed to see for ourselves. We headed toward the edge of town, where the Jenkins' house stood. It was a modest place, with a white picket fence and a well-tended garden. But today, it was eerily quiet. No sign of life. The curtains were drawn, the door locked.

Ben tried knocking, but there was no answer.

"This is so weird," he muttered, stepping back. "Where could they have gone?"

I looked around, my heart pounding. "Let's check the Thompsons' place."

We hurried down the street, passing other houses that seemed just as deserted. The Thompsons' house was just a few blocks away, but when we got there, it was the same story—no one home, no sign of where they might have gone.

Panic began to bubble up in my chest. "What's happening, Ben? This isn't normal."

He didn't answer right away. He just stared at the house, his face pale. "I don't know. But we need to find out."

We spent the rest of the afternoon checking house after house, each one as empty as the last. By the time the sun began to set, we had a list of over a dozen families that had vanished without a trace.

It wasn't just a coincidence. Something was taking people—whole families—and no one seemed to know why.

As the darkness closed in, Ben and I stood on the empty street, the weight of the day's discoveries pressing down on us.

"We need to tell someone," I said, my voice barely more than a whisper.

Ben nodded. "Yeah. But who? And what do we even say?"

I didn't have an answer. All I knew was that Hollowbrook was changing, and if we didn't figure out what was going on, more people would disappear.

And maybe, just maybe, we would be next.

THREE

THE FIRST CLUE

The next morning, Hollowbrook felt even more off-kilter. The usual buzz of the town was replaced by a tense quiet, the kind that sinks into your bones and stays there. People hurried along the streets, heads down, whispers floating through the air like fragments of some collective nightmare they were trying to piece together.

I met Ben at the corner again, and it was clear he hadn't slept much either. His eyes were dark and tired, his usual easygoing smile nowhere to be found.

"We need to figure this out," I said, skipping any pleasantries. "Before more people vanish."

Ben nodded, pulling his jacket tighter around him. "Yeah. But where do we even start?"

I had been thinking about that all night. "The woods. Whoever—or whatever—was standing there yesterday, they might know something. It's the only lead we have."

Ben hesitated, glancing toward the edge of town where the forest loomed, dark and mysterious. The woods had always been a place of whispered stories and childhood dares, but this was different. This wasn't a game.

"Alright," he said finally, his voice steady but his eyes betraying his uncertainty. "Let's check it out."

The walk to the woods felt longer than usual, every step weighed down by the unknown. The trees stood tall and silent, their branches twisting together to form a canopy that blocked out most of the light. As we stepped into the shadows, the air grew colder, the faint smell of damp earth and pine needles filling our senses.

We didn't speak much as we moved deeper into the forest, the quiet only broken by the occasional snap of a twig or the rustle of leaves. Each sound made my heart race, every shadow playing tricks on my mind. I kept expecting to see the figure again, standing just beyond the trees, watching us.

But the woods seemed empty.

"We're not going to find anything," Ben muttered after a while, frustration creeping into his voice. "It's just trees and more trees."

I was starting to think he was right when something caught my eye—a faint trail leading off to the side, barely visible under the thick underbrush. It wasn't much, but it was enough to make me pause.

"Wait," I said, pointing. "Over there."

Ben followed my gaze, his brow furrowing. "You think someone's been walking here?"

I nodded. "Let's check it out."

We followed the trail, pushing aside branches and stepping carefully over the roots that snaked across the ground. The further we went, the more certain I became that this wasn't just an animal path. The way the underbrush was trampled down suggested that someone—or something—had come through here recently.

The trail led us to a small clearing, and in the center of it stood an old, crumbling stone structure. It looked like it had been there for centuries, moss and ivy clinging to its weathered surface. A low, circular wall surrounded a dark hole in the ground—a well, or what used to be one.

Ben walked up to it, peering over the edge. “What do you think this is?”

I joined him, feeling a chill as I looked down into the darkness. “I don’t know. But it feels... important.”

As we stood there, a faint sound reached us from the depths of the well—a soft, echoing whisper that sent a shiver down my spine. It was too faint to make out the words, but it was there, and it was definitely not the wind.

“You hear that?” I asked, my voice barely more than a breath.

Ben nodded slowly, his eyes wide. “Yeah. What is that?”

We exchanged a look, the same thought running through both our minds. Whatever was down there, it was connected to the disappearances. We had found the first clue.

But now we had to decide what to do with it.

“We should tell someone,” Ben said, stepping back from the well. “The police, maybe.”

“And say what?” I replied. “That we found an old well in the woods that’s whispering at us? They’ll think we’re crazy.”

He sighed, running a hand through his hair. “So, what then? We just leave it?”

“No,” I said firmly. “We need to find out what’s down there. It’s the only way we’ll get answers.”

Ben hesitated, clearly torn. He wasn’t wrong to be cautious; whatever was happening in Hollowbrook was bigger than us, and we were in over our heads. But we couldn't just walk away. Not now.

"Alright," he said finally, his voice steadying. "But we need a plan. We can't just jump in."

I nodded, already thinking ahead. "We'll come back tonight. Bring flashlights, rope, anything we might need."

Ben gave a reluctant smile. "You really think we're going to find something down there?"

"I do," I said. "And I think it's going to help us understand what's happening to Hollowbrook."

As we turned to head back to town, the weight of what we had discovered settled over me. The well was just the beginning. Whatever lay beneath it, it held the answers we were looking for.

We just had to be brave enough to face it.

FOUR

A Descent into Darkness

That evening, the sky over Hollowbrook was painted in hues of deep orange and purple as the sun dipped below the horizon. But for Ben and me, the beauty of the sunset was lost in the growing tension of what lay ahead. The discovery of the old well in the woods had set something in motion, and we both knew there was no turning back.

We met at my house just after dinner, our backpacks filled with everything we thought we might need—flashlights, rope, a first aid kit, even some snacks in case we were out longer than expected. It felt strange, like we were heading off on some kind of expedition, but the weight of the situation pressed down on us, reminding us this was no ordinary adventure.

"You ready?" Ben asked, adjusting his backpack as we stepped onto the front porch.

I nodded, my heart pounding. "Yeah. Let's go."

The streets of Hollowbrook were eerily quiet as we made our way toward the woods. The usual hum of evening activity was missing, replaced by a stillness that only deepened my sense of unease. It was as if the entire town was holding its breath, waiting for something to happen.

When we reached the edge of the forest, the last rays of sunlight were fading, casting long shadows among the trees. We turned on our flashlights, the beams cutting through the encroaching darkness as we followed the now-familiar path to the clearing.

The woods felt different at night—darker, more alive somehow. The usual rustling of leaves and distant calls of night creatures seemed amplified, each sound a reminder that we were venturing into unknown territory. I kept my focus on the trail ahead, trying to ignore the way the darkness seemed to close in around us.

When we finally reached the clearing, the old stone structure loomed before us, its weathered surface casting long, ominous shadows. The well seemed to breathe in the dark, the faint whispering from earlier now barely audible but still there, lingering just on the edge of hearing.

"We're really doing this," Ben muttered, more to himself than to me.

"We have to," I replied, stepping toward the well. "This might be the only way to figure out what's going on."

We secured the rope to a sturdy tree nearby, testing it a few times to make sure it would hold. Ben went first, descending slowly into the dark maw of the well. The rope creaked softly as it bore his weight, the sound echoing eerily off the stone walls.

"Careful," I called down, my voice bouncing off the stones.

"Yeah, I got it," Ben replied, his voice tense but steady. "It's not as deep as I thought. I can see the bottom."

A moment later, his feet touched down, and he called up to me. "Your turn."

I took a deep breath, gripping the rope tightly as I swung my legs over the edge and began to lower myself down. The air inside the well was cool and damp, the scent of moss and earth filling my nose. The darkness pressed in around me, but I focused on the rope, counting each hand over hand movement until my feet finally met solid ground.

The bottom of the well was surprisingly spacious, more like a small underground chamber than the narrow pit I had expected. The stone walls were slick with moisture, and the floor was covered in a thin layer of dirt and debris.

Ben shone his flashlight around, revealing more of the chamber. There was a narrow passage leading further into the earth, the walls carved out of rough stone. The whispering was louder here, more distinct, though the words were still just out of reach.

"Where do you think this leads?" Ben asked, his voice low, almost reverent in the confined space.

"Only one way to find out," I said, my own voice echoing slightly in the chamber.

We moved cautiously into the passage, the narrow tunnel forcing us to walk single file. The air grew colder the further we went, the whispering growing louder with each step. It wasn't just a sound anymore—it was a presence, something ancient and knowing that seemed to wrap around us, urging us deeper into the darkness.

The tunnel eventually opened into another chamber, this one larger and more ornate. Strange symbols were etched into the walls, their meanings lost to time, and in the center of the room stood a stone pedestal, its surface cracked and worn with age.

"What is this place?" Ben whispered, his flashlight sweeping over the ancient carvings.

"I don't know," I replied, stepping closer to the pedestal. "But it's been here a long time."

The whispering was louder here, almost deafening in its intensity. It seemed to emanate from the very walls, the air thrumming with energy. I reached out, my fingers brushing against the surface of the pedestal, and in that instant, the whispering stopped.

Silence. Complete and utter silence.

Ben and I exchanged a glance, the sudden absence of sound more unsettling than the whispering had ever been. The air felt charged, as if the room itself was waiting for something.

Before we could react, a low rumble shook the chamber, dust and small stones raining down from the ceiling. The symbols on the walls began to glow faintly, a soft, pulsating light that bathed the room in an eerie glow.

"We need to get out of here," Ben said urgently, his eyes wide with fear.

But I couldn't move. Something about the pedestal held me in place, a force I couldn't see but could feel deep within me.

Then, just as suddenly as it started, the rumbling stopped. The light from the symbols faded, and the whispering returned, softer now, almost gentle.

I stumbled back from the pedestal, my heart racing. Whatever we had just witnessed, it was connected to the disappearances in Hollowbrook. I was sure of it.

"We need to get back to the surface," I said, my voice trembling. "And we need to figure out what this all means."

Ben nodded, already moving toward the tunnel. "Agreed. But we have to be careful. I don't think this place wants us here."

As we made our way back through the passage, the weight of what we had discovered pressed down on me. We were standing on the edge of something vast and ancient, something that had been hidden beneath Hollowbrook for who knows how long.

And now, it was waking up.

FIVE

The Whispering Truth

The trek back to the surface felt longer, the weight of our discovery pressing down on me like a heavy blanket. My mind raced with questions as we climbed out of the well, the quiet of the night surrounding us like an unwelcome companion. Ben was just as shaken, his silence a stark contrast to his usual chatter.

Once we were back above ground, we didn't stop to talk. We needed to get away from the well, away from the oppressive feeling that something—or someone—was watching us from the shadows. The forest seemed darker than before, the trees towering like silent sentinels, hiding secrets we had only just begun to uncover.

We didn't speak until we were back at the edge of the woods, the lights of Hollowbrook flickering faintly in the distance.

"We need to tell someone," Ben said, breaking the silence. His voice was shaky, but there was a determination in his eyes. "This isn't just about the town disappearing. This is something... bigger."

I nodded, though I wasn't sure who we could trust. "We can't go to the police with this. They'll think we're crazy. We need proof."

Ben sighed, running a hand through his hair. "Proof. Right. And how exactly do we get that?"

I didn't have an answer. The symbols, the whispering, the pedestal—none of it made sense. But I knew one thing: whatever was happening in Hollowbrook, it was connected to the well and that strange underground chamber.

"We'll figure it out," I said, trying to sound more confident than I felt. "But we need to stay calm. Panic won't help anyone."

Ben nodded slowly. "Okay. So, what's the plan?"

I thought for a moment, the gears in my mind turning. "We need to research those symbols. Maybe they're part of some ancient language or ritual. If we can figure out what they mean, we might get some answers."

Ben frowned. "And where do we start with that? It's not like we can just Google 'weird glowing symbols in an old well.'"

He had a point, but I wasn't ready to give up. "The library. There's got to be something there about Hollowbrook's history, maybe even something about the well."

It wasn't much of a plan, but it was all we had. Ben agreed, and we made a pact to meet at the library first thing in the morning.

That night, sleep didn't come easily. My dreams were filled with images of the well, the glowing symbols, and the whispering that seemed to echo in my ears even as I tossed and turned in my bed. I woke up more exhausted than when I had gone to sleep, but the urgency of our mission pushed me out of bed and toward the library.

Ben was already there when I arrived, his face buried in a thick book that looked like it hadn't been opened in decades.

"Anything?" I asked, sliding into the chair across from him.

He shook his head, frustration etched into his features. "Nothing so far. Just a lot of old town records and some boring history stuff."

I grabbed a stack of books from the nearby table, determined to find something useful. We spent hours flipping through pages, our fingers tracing over faded text and ancient diagrams. The more we read, the more it seemed like we were chasing shadows, the truth always just out of reach.

Then, just as I was about to give up, I found it—a book that looked different from the others. It was smaller, bound in worn leather, with no title on the cover. I opened it carefully, the pages brittle and yellowed with age.

The text was handwritten, the ink faded but still legible. It wasn't in English, but the symbols—those strange, glowing symbols from the well—were there, scattered throughout the pages. My heart pounded as I realized we had found something.

"Ben," I whispered, pushing the book toward him. "Look at this."

He leaned over, his eyes widening as he scanned the pages. "That's it. Those are the symbols."

We both stared at the book, a mix of excitement and fear swirling in our chests. This was our proof, but it also raised more questions than it answered. Who wrote this book? What did the symbols mean? And how were they connected to the disappearances in Hollowbrook?

Ben flipped through the pages, stopping at a passage that seemed to be a translation of the symbols. "It's some kind of ancient language," he murmured. "Something about a 'veil between worlds' and 'guardians of the gateway.'"

The words sent a chill down my spine. "A gateway? You think the well is some kind of portal?"

Ben didn't answer right away, his brow furrowed in concentration. "Maybe. Or maybe it's just a metaphor. But whatever it is, it's old. And powerful."

We kept reading, piecing together fragments of information from the book. It spoke of a town built on sacred ground, a place where the veil between worlds was thin. The well was a focal point, a place where energies converged, and the symbols were part of a ritual to keep something sealed away.

"This... this is crazy," Ben said, leaning back in his chair. "We're talking about ancient rituals and gateways to other worlds. How is this even possible?"

I didn't have an answer. All I knew was that we were in over our heads. But we couldn't stop now. We had to see this through, no matter where it led.

"We need to go back," I said, closing the book gently. "There's more to the well than we saw. We have to find out what's really down there."

Ben hesitated, fear flickering in his eyes. "Are you sure? This feels... dangerous."

I met his gaze, my resolve hardening. "I'm sure. If we don't, more people will disappear. We have to stop it."

He nodded, though I could see the worry in his expression. "Alright. But we need to be careful. Whatever's down there, it's been hidden for a reason."

As we left the library, the weight of our discovery pressed down on me. The book had given us a glimpse into the truth, but it also made one thing clear: we were dealing with forces far beyond our understanding.

And the only way to save Hollowbrook was to face those forces head-on.

SIX

UNVEILING THE PAST

The weight of our discovery from the library stayed with us as we walked back toward the woods. The book had revealed fragments of a forgotten history, stories of a veil between worlds, and a ritual to seal something away. It felt surreal, like we had stumbled into a story that was never meant to be unearthed.

The afternoon sun hung low in the sky, casting long shadows that danced across the ground as the wind rustled through the trees. Despite the beauty of the day, an unease settled over me, like the calm before a storm.

"We should go over what we know," Ben said, breaking the silence as we reached the edge of the woods. "Make sure we're not missing anything."

I nodded, grateful for the suggestion. The more we understood, the better prepared we'd be for whatever lay ahead. We found a quiet spot just inside the forest and sat down on a fallen log, the sound of the rustling leaves our only company.

"Okay," I started, pulling the old book from my backpack and flipping to the pages we'd marked. "So, the well is part of some kind of ancient ritual to keep something sealed away. The symbols are part of that ritual."

Ben leaned in, his eyes scanning the page. "And the book mentioned a veil between worlds. If the well is a gateway or something, maybe the people who built it knew about whatever's on the other side."

"Exactly," I agreed, my fingers tracing the faded symbols. "But what happened to them? Why is the well hidden now? And why are people disappearing?"

Ben exhaled slowly, running a hand through his hair. "Maybe the ritual failed, or it's wearing off. And if it is a gateway, maybe something's coming through."

The thought sent a shiver down my spine. "But why now? The well's been there for centuries."

We sat in silence for a moment, the enormity of what we were facing sinking in. Whatever was happening, it had been set in motion long before we were born, and now it was reaching its climax.

"There's one more thing," I said, my voice hesitant. "The whispering. It's like it's trying to tell us something."

Ben nodded, his expression thoughtful. "Yeah, but it's not just random noise. It feels... deliberate."

I flipped to a passage in the book that described the symbols as a language, a way to communicate with the forces beyond the veil. "What if the whispering is a message? Maybe it's connected to the symbols. If we can figure out what it's saying, we might understand what's happening."

Ben's eyes lit up with a mix of excitement and fear. "But how do we do that? We can't just sit and listen to it all day."

"We'll need to go back to the well," I said, the words feeling heavier than I expected. "If it's a message, we need to hear it clearly, away from the noise of the town."

Ben hesitated, the worry evident on his face. "Are you sure that's a good idea? What if it's dangerous?"

I met his gaze, my resolve firming. "It's a risk, but we don't have a choice. We need to understand what's going on, and this might be the only way."

He nodded reluctantly. "Alright. But we need to be careful. If it starts feeling wrong, we get out of there."

Agreed, we packed up the book and made our way deeper into the forest, the path to the well now familiar. The sun was beginning to set, casting a golden glow through the trees, but the beauty of the scene was lost on us. We were focused, our minds set on uncovering the truth.

When we reached the clearing, the well stood there, silent and imposing. The whispering was faint, barely audible over the rustling leaves, but it was there, persistent.

We set up near the well, sitting cross-legged with the book between us. The symbols seemed to glow faintly in the dim light, a reminder of the power they held.

"Okay," Ben said, taking a deep breath. "Let's do this."

We closed our eyes, focusing on the whispering, letting it wash over us. At first, it was just a jumble of sounds, but as we listened, patterns began to emerge—words, phrases, meanings that were just out of reach.

"It's like... a warning," I said slowly, the realization dawning on me. "It's telling us something's coming. Something we need to stop."

Ben's eyes snapped open, his expression serious. "A warning? Like what?"

I flipped through the book, searching for a passage that might help us decipher the message. My fingers landed on a page describing the guardians of the gateway, beings tasked with protecting the world from whatever lay beyond the veil.

"The guardians," I murmured, my mind racing. "They were supposed to keep the gateway closed, but if the ritual is failing, maybe they can't anymore."

Ben's face paled. "So, the whispering is from them? They're trying to tell us to stop whatever's coming through?"

I nodded, the weight of the revelation settling over us. "And if we don't, more people will disappear. Maybe even the whole town."

We sat in silence, the gravity of our task pressing down on us. We were just two kids, facing forces we could barely comprehend, but we knew we had to try. Hollowbrook's fate depended on it.

Ben broke the silence, his voice filled with determination. "Then we need to find out how to complete the ritual. How to reinforce the seal."

I nodded, flipping through the book for any clues. "There has to be something in here. We'll figure it out. We have to."

As the sun dipped below the horizon, casting the forest in shadow, we huddled over the book, the whispering guiding us toward the answers we sought. The past was unveiling itself, piece by piece, and we were determined to uncover the truth, no matter the cost.

SEVEN

ECHOES OF THE ANCIENTS

The forest was eerily quiet as Ben and I made our way back to my house, the old leather-bound book clutched tightly in my hands. The whispering from the well still echoed faintly in my mind, a constant reminder of the message we had yet to fully decipher. The sun had long set, and the darkness that enveloped Hollowbrook seemed thicker, heavier, as if the town itself was holding its breath.

"We need to figure this out, fast," Ben said, his voice cutting through the silence. "If the ritual fails completely, who knows what'll happen."

I nodded, the weight of our discovery pressing down on me. "We're running out of time. We have to understand the ritual and the symbols before it's too late."

Once we were inside, we spread the book out on my kitchen table, the dim light from the overhead lamp casting long shadows across the pages. The ancient symbols, drawn in fading ink, seemed almost alive under the flickering light, their meanings just out of reach.

Ben grabbed a notebook and a pen, ready to take notes. "Alright, let's go over everything again. The whispering, the symbols, the well... there's got to be a connection we're missing."

I flipped through the pages, my fingers brushing over the delicate parchment. "The book mentioned guardians, remember? They were supposed to protect the gateway. But if they're sending warnings now, it means something's gone wrong."

Ben scribbled down notes, his brow furrowed in concentration. "Right. And the well—it's the gateway. The symbols are part of the ritual that keeps it sealed. So, we need to understand the symbols to figure out how to fix the seal."

The symbols were complex, interwoven with lines and shapes that seemed to shift as I stared at them. It was as if they held a secret language, one that we had to decode to save Hollowbrook.

"Maybe we should try to match them with the whispering," I suggested, tapping the page. "If the whispering is a message, maybe the symbols correspond to it somehow."

Ben nodded. "Good idea. But how do we translate it? The book is written in some ancient language we don't understand."

I thought for a moment, then grabbed my phone. "There's got to be something online about ancient languages and symbols. Maybe we can find a match or at least get a clue."

We spent the next few hours scouring the internet, searching for anything that resembled the symbols from the book. It was slow going, each page filled with countless images and texts that didn't quite fit. Frustration bubbled up inside me as the minutes ticked by, but I pushed it down, focusing on the task at hand.

Finally, Ben's voice broke through the silence. "Hey, look at this."

I leaned over, peering at his screen. He had found an article about ancient languages and symbols used in rituals to seal portals between worlds. The symbols looked strikingly similar to the ones in our book.

"This could be it," I whispered, excitement mixing with fear. "It talks about using symbols to create a barrier, to reinforce the seal on a gateway."

Ben scrolled down, his eyes scanning the text. "It says here that the symbols have to be drawn in a specific order, like a pattern. If we can figure out the right sequence, we can reinforce the seal."

I grabbed the book, flipping to the page with the symbols. "Then we need to figure out the sequence. It's like solving a puzzle."

We compared the symbols from the book with the ones in the article, searching for clues that would lead us to the correct order. The process was painstaking, each symbol needing to be matched carefully, but slowly, a pattern began to emerge.

"I think I've got it," Ben said, his voice tense with concentration. He pointed to the page. "Look, these symbols are repeated in the book, but in different orders. If we follow the sequence from the article, it might work."

I traced the symbols with my finger, trying to commit the pattern to memory. "It's worth a shot. But we need to be sure. If we mess this up, it could make things worse."

Ben nodded solemnly. "We'll double-check everything. We can't afford any mistakes."

The hours slipped by as we worked, the quiet of the house broken only by the sound of pages turning and the occasional muttered curse when we hit a snag. The weight of what we were doing pressed down on us, the knowledge that the fate of Hollowbrook rested on our ability to decode an ancient language and perform a ritual we barely understood.

Finally, we had the sequence, a series of symbols that we hoped would reinforce the seal on the well. I leaned back in my chair, exhaustion washing over me, but there was no time to rest.

"We need to go back to the well," I said, my voice hoarse. "We have to do this before the ritual fails completely."

Ben stood up, stretching his arms. "Yeah. The sooner, the better. Let's gather what we need and head out."

We packed up the book and the notes, our hearts pounding with a mix of fear and determination. The forest was waiting, the well was waiting, and so was whatever lay beyond the veil.

As we stepped outside, the night air was cool against my skin, the stars above twinkling faintly. The quiet of the town was almost comforting, but I knew that it was just the calm before the storm.

"Ready?" Ben asked, his voice steady despite the tremor in his hands.

I nodded, gripping the book tightly. "Ready. Let's save Hollowbrook."

And with that, we set off into the night, the echoes of the ancients guiding us toward the well and the truth that lay within.

EIGHT

A Race Against Time

The night enveloped us as we made our way back to the well, the ancient book clutched tightly in my arms. The forest, usually so familiar and comforting, now seemed to close in around us, the trees standing like silent sentinels in the darkness. The weight of what we were about to do pressed down on me, each step heavier than the last.

Ben walked beside me, his flashlight cutting through the gloom, casting long, flickering shadows that danced at the edge of my vision. Neither of us spoke, the gravity of our mission silencing any attempts at conversation. The symbols, the whispers, the ancient ritual—we were finally about to face it all head-on.

The path to the well was steeped in shadows, the moon hidden behind thick clouds that blotted out the stars. The forest floor was soft beneath our feet, muffling our steps as we moved deeper into the woods. My heart pounded in my chest, each beat a reminder of the ticking clock we were racing against.

When we reached the clearing, the well stood before us, a dark, looming presence against the backdrop of the forest. The whispering was louder now, a low hum that seemed to rise from the depths of the earth, wrapping around us in an eerie embrace. It was both a warning and a plea, urging us to hurry.

Ben set down his backpack, pulling out the notebook with the sequence of symbols we had painstakingly decoded. "We need to get this right the first time," he said, his voice steady but his hands trembling slightly. "There might not be a second chance."

I nodded, opening the old book to the page with the symbols. "Let's go over it one more time. We can't afford any mistakes."

We huddled over the book and the notebook, the flashlight casting a pale glow over the pages. The symbols seemed to shimmer in the light, as if they were alive, waiting for us to unlock their secrets.

"The sequence," Ben murmured, pointing to the first symbol. "We start here."

I followed his finger, my breath catching in my throat. The symbol was familiar, etched into my memory from the hours we had spent decoding it. I traced it with my finger, the lines smooth under my touch.

"And then this one," I added, moving to the next symbol. "We follow the pattern exactly as we figured it out."

Ben nodded, his eyes meeting mine. "Are you ready?"

I took a deep breath, trying to steady the racing of my heart. "As ready as I'll ever be."

We moved to the edge of the well, the whispering growing louder, almost frantic, as if urging us to hurry. The ancient stone was cold beneath my fingertips, the weight of centuries pressing down on it—and on us.

Ben placed the notebook beside the well, its pages fluttering in the night breeze. "We'll draw the symbols here," he said, his voice barely above a whisper. "Right where the others were faded."

I nodded, pulling out the chalk we had brought. My hands trembled as I began to draw the first symbol, the lines crisp and precise against the aged stone. The whispering seemed to intensify with each stroke, the air around us growing colder.

Ben followed, his hand steady as he traced the next symbol. We worked in silence, the weight of the ritual pressing down on us. Each symbol felt like a key, unlocking a part of the ancient seal that had been in place for centuries.

As we drew the final symbol, a sudden gust of wind tore through the clearing, extinguishing our flashlight. Darkness swallowed us, the whispering now a cacophony of voices rising from the depths of the well.

"Ben!" I called out, panic rising in my chest. "The light!"

"I'm on it!" he replied, fumbling in the dark to relight the flashlight.

When the beam flickered back to life, we both gasped. The symbols we had drawn were glowing faintly, a soft, pulsating light that seemed to breathe with life. The whispering had changed, no longer frantic but rhythmic, almost like a chant.

"It's working," Ben said, awe in his voice. "The seal... it's being reinforced."

But even as relief washed over me, a new sound emerged from the well—a low, rumbling growl that sent chills down my spine. The ground beneath us trembled, small rocks shifting as the ancient forces within the well stirred.

"We have to finish this," I said urgently. "The last part of the ritual!"

Ben nodded, flipping through the notebook. "The final step... we need to speak the words from the book. The ones written next to the sequence."

I grabbed the book, my eyes scanning the faded text. The words were in the ancient language, their meanings lost to time, but their power palpable. I took a deep breath, my voice steady as I began to read them aloud.

The air around us seemed to thicken, the whispering rising to a crescendo. The glowing symbols brightened, their light cutting through the darkness, illuminating the well and the surrounding trees.

Ben joined me, his voice strong as we spoke the words together, our voices merging with the ancient chant that echoed from the depths of the well. The rumbling grew louder, the ground shaking beneath our feet as the forces within the well pushed against the seal.

And then, suddenly, it stopped.

The whispering ceased, the rumbling quieted, and the forest fell into an eerie silence. The glow from the symbols faded, leaving us in the dim light of the flashlight.

We stood there, breathless, the weight of the moment sinking in. The seal had held, the ritual completed, but the silence was heavy, filled with unspoken questions.

"Did it work?" Ben asked, his voice barely a whisper.

I nodded slowly, though uncertainty gnawed at the edges of my mind. "I think so. The seal is reinforced. For now."

But even as the words left my lips, I knew our journey wasn't over. The forces we had encountered were ancient and powerful, and their whispers hinted at a deeper mystery yet to be uncovered.

"We need to get back," I said, the urgency returning. "We need to figure out what's next. This isn't over."

Ben agreed, and we gathered our things, the ancient book once again our guide. As we left the clearing, the well stood silent behind us, its secrets buried for now—but not forgotten.

The race against time had paused, but the echoes of the ancients still lingered, a reminder that the veil between worlds was thinner than ever. And Hollowbrook's fate was far from sealed.

NINE

The Calm Before the Storm

The walk back to town felt longer than usual, the weight of what Ben and I had just done pressing heavily on our shoulders. The forest, usually a haven of tranquility, seemed different now—darker, quieter, as if it was holding its breath along with us. The whispering had stopped, the well sealed for now, but the sense of unease lingered.

Ben was the first to break the silence. "Do you think it'll hold?"

I sighed, my gaze fixed on the path ahead. "I don't know. The book said the ritual was supposed to reinforce the seal, but we're dealing with forces we barely understand. We might've bought some time, but that's it."

The streetlights of Hollowbrook came into view, their soft glow cutting through the darkness. The town was eerily quiet, most people having retreated to the safety of their homes. It was as if the town itself knew something was wrong, even if the townsfolk couldn't put their finger on it.

We reached my house, the porch light flickering slightly in the cool night breeze. I unlocked the door, and we stepped inside, the familiar warmth of home wrapping around us like a blanket. But even here, the weight of our discovery followed us.

Ben collapsed onto the couch, running a hand through his hair. "So, what now? We just wait and see if the seal holds?"

I shook my head, setting the ancient book on the coffee table. "We can't just wait. We need to understand what we're dealing with. There's got to be more in this book—something we missed, some clue about what's beyond the well."

Ben leaned forward, his elbows resting on his knees. "The guardians. The book mentioned them. Maybe they're the key to understanding all of this."

I opened the book again, flipping through the pages we had skimmed over earlier. The guardians were supposed to protect the gateway, to keep whatever was on the other side from crossing over. But if they were sending warnings now, it meant something had gone terribly wrong.

"We need to find out what happened to the guardians," I said, my fingers tracing the faded text. "If they've been compromised, it could explain why the seal is failing."

Ben nodded, his eyes narrowing in thought. "But how do we do that? The book is ancient, and we don't even know where to start."

I leaned back, my mind racing. "The well was built centuries ago. There's got to be more information somewhere—old records, maybe something in the town's history."

Ben stood up, pacing the room. "The library. They have archives, right? Old newspapers, town records. We should check there."

"Good idea," I agreed, closing the book. "But we'll need to be careful. We don't know who or what might be watching us now."

The thought sent a shiver down my spine, but I pushed it aside. We had come too far to back down now. The fate of Hollowbrook was at stake, and we were the only ones who could do anything about it.

We spent the rest of the night poring over the book, looking for any additional clues that might help us understand the ritual and the forces at play. The ancient language was difficult to decipher, but the more we studied, the more patterns began to emerge.

By the time the first rays of dawn crept through the window, we were both exhausted, but we had a plan. The library would be our next stop, and we would delve into Hollowbrook's history to find the answers we needed.

Ben yawned, stretching his arms above his head. "We should get some rest before we head to the library. We'll need to be sharp."

I nodded, closing the book and setting it aside. "Yeah. A few hours of sleep, then we'll head out."

We retreated to our respective rooms, the weight of the night's events pressing down on us. Sleep came fitfully, my mind filled with images of glowing symbols, whispering voices, and a well that held more secrets than we could imagine.

When I woke, the sun was higher in the sky, casting a golden light across my room. I rubbed my eyes, the fatigue from the night before still lingering, but the determination burning brighter than ever.

I met Ben in the kitchen, the smell of coffee filling the air. He handed me a cup, his eyes heavy with sleep but filled with resolve.

"Ready?" he asked, his voice steady despite the exhaustion.

I nodded, taking a sip of the coffee. "Ready. Let's uncover the truth."

We set out for the library, the town still quiet in the early morning light. The streets were empty, the usual buzz of life absent, as if Hollowbrook itself was holding its breath, waiting for what was to come.

The library loomed before us, its doors a gateway to the past. We stepped inside, the familiar smell of old books and dust greeting us. The librarian, an elderly woman with kind eyes, glanced up from her desk and gave us a warm smile.

"Good morning, dears," she said, her voice soft. "What brings you to the library so early?"

Ben stepped forward, his expression serious. "We're doing some research on the town's history. We need to look at the old records and archives."

The librarian nodded, gesturing to a door at the back of the room. "You'll find what you need in the archives. Let me know if you need any help."

We thanked her and made our way to the archives, the door creaking open to reveal rows of shelves filled with dusty books, old newspapers, and yellowed documents. The weight of history pressed down on us, each artifact a piece of Hollowbrook's past.

Ben and I exchanged a glance, the gravity of our task sinking in. "Let's get to work," he said, his voice low. "The answers are here somewhere."

We began to search, our hands moving quickly over the documents, our eyes scanning for anything that might give us a clue about the guardians, the well, and the forces we were up against. The clock was ticking, and the storm was coming. We had to be ready.

TEN

GUARDIANS OF THE PAST

Chapter 10: Guardians of the Past

The air inside the library's archives was thick with the scent of old paper and history. The dim lighting from the overhead bulbs cast long shadows across the rows of shelves, giving the room an almost sacred feel. Ben and I stood at the threshold, the weight of our mission pressing down on us like a heavy cloak. Somewhere in this room, buried within the pages of forgotten records, lay the answers we desperately needed.

"We should split up," I suggested, my voice barely a whisper in the quiet room. "We'll cover more ground that way."

Ben nodded, his eyes scanning the rows of shelves. "Good idea. We're looking for anything about the well, the guardians, or any strange events in the town's past."

We each picked a side of the room and got to work, pulling out old newspapers, journals, and dusty tomes, scanning them for clues. The hum of the fluorescent lights was the only sound, punctuated by the occasional rustle of turning pages.

Time seemed to stretch as we combed through the records. Every now and then, I'd glance over at Ben, who was just as engrossed in his search. The sheer volume of information was overwhelming, but we couldn't afford to miss anything.

Hours passed, and my eyes were beginning to blur from reading the faded text when I finally stumbled upon something. It was a small, leather-bound journal, its pages yellowed with age. The handwriting was meticulous, the ink slightly faded but still legible. I flipped to a random page, my heart skipping a beat as I read the words: *"The guardians have fallen, and the seal weakens."*

"Ben," I called out, my voice urgent. "I found something."

He hurried over, peering over my shoulder at the journal. "What is it?"

I pointed to the passage, my finger trembling slightly. "It's a journal entry from someone who knew about the well and the guardians. It mentions the seal weakening."

Ben's eyes widened. "That's exactly what we need. Who wrote this?"

I turned to the front of the journal, searching for a name. "It's written by someone named Elijah Turner. Do you recognize that name?"

Ben shook his head, frowning. "No, but if he knew about the guardians, he must've been important."

I flipped through the pages, skimming the entries. "There's more. Listen to this: *'The whispers grow louder each night. The guardians, once strong, now falter. We must act before it's too late.'*"

Ben's brow furrowed. "The whispers... just like what we've been hearing. This Elijah knew what was coming. Maybe he knew how to stop it."

"We need to read this whole journal," I said, clutching the book tightly. "It might have the answers we're looking for."

We settled at a nearby table, the journal between us. As we read, a picture of Hollowbrook's past began to emerge—one filled with secrets, ancient rituals, and a group of protectors who had dedicated their lives to keeping the town safe from the forces beyond the well.

Elijah Turner was one of the last known guardians, his journal chronicling the slow decay of their power and the rising threat of the entities trapped on the other side. He described how the seal had held for generations, strengthened by the guardians' rituals. But as their numbers dwindled, so did the strength of the seal.

"We're seeing history repeat itself," Ben murmured, his eyes scanning the pages. "The guardians failed before, and the seal broke. That's what we're facing now."

I nodded, my mind racing. "But Elijah must've tried to find a way to stop it. There has to be something in here about how they fought back, how they tried to repair the seal."

We continued reading, our focus unbroken even as the day wore on. The journal spoke of desperate measures, of rituals performed under moonlight, and of sacrifices made to keep the town safe. Elijah's words were heavy with regret and fear, but also with determination.

As we reached the final pages, Elijah's tone shifted. He spoke of a final attempt to contact the remaining guardians, to rally them for one last stand. But the entries ended abruptly, leaving us with more questions than answers.

"It just... stops," I said, frustration creeping into my voice. "What happened to him? To the guardians?"

Ben rubbed his temples, deep in thought. "Maybe the library has other records about Elijah. We need to know how his story ended."

We returned to the shelves, our search now focused on finding any mention of Elijah Turner. It didn't take long before we stumbled upon a collection of old town council records, one of which mentioned an incident at the well.

Ben's finger traced the faded text. "Here it is. *'Elijah Turner, last of the guardians, was lost during the final sealing ritual. The well was secured, but at a great cost.'*"

I felt a lump form in my throat. "He gave his life to protect Hollowbrook."

Ben nodded solemnly. "And now it's up to us to continue what he started."

We sat in silence for a moment, the enormity of our task sinking in. The guardians were gone, and the town had forgotten its own history. But the threat remained, and it was growing stronger.

"We need to find out how Elijah performed that final ritual," I said, determination hardening my voice. "If it worked once, maybe it can work again."

Ben agreed, and we gathered our notes and the journal, ready to face whatever came next. The guardians of the past had fought to keep Hollowbrook safe, and now it was our turn to take up their mantle. The calm before the storm was over, and the fight was just beginning.

ELEVEN

The Secret Beneath the Well

The next morning, a thick fog had settled over Hollowbrook, muffling the sounds of the waking town. The world outside felt distant and unreal, as though it were just as trapped in time as we were. Ben and I stood by the kitchen table, the remnants of a quick breakfast pushed aside in favor of the journal and our scattered notes.

We had spent most of the night trying to piece together Elijah Turner's final ritual. The text was cryptic, filled with symbols and ancient phrases that we could barely understand. Yet, there was a pattern, a rhythm that suggested a deeper meaning.

Ben tapped his pen against the table, breaking the silence. "We need to decipher this before the seal weakens any further. The journal hinted at something beneath the well—something that might help."

I nodded, my eyes on the faded lines of text. "Elijah mentioned the 'source of the seal's power' hidden beneath the well. If we can find it, we might stand a chance at strengthening the seal."

"But getting to it is the problem," Ben said, leaning back in his chair. "The well is ancient, and it's been sealed off for generations. If we're going to do this, we need to be prepared for anything."

We both knew what he meant. The well wasn't just a gateway; it was a prison. Whatever was trapped on the other side would not welcome our interference.

By midday, we had gathered what we thought we'd need—flashlights, ropes, and anything else that could help us navigate the unknown depths. The fog had lifted slightly, but the oppressive atmosphere remained, as though the town itself knew we were about to cross a line that should never be crossed.

We reached the well, the old stone structure standing as silent and foreboding as ever. The runes we had carved the day before were still visible, their glow dimmed but not gone. I ran my hand over them, feeling the faint hum of the ancient magic that still lingered.

"Ready?" Ben asked, his voice steady but his eyes betraying his anxiety.

I took a deep breath, steeling myself. "As ready as we'll ever be."

We tied the ropes securely, anchoring them to a sturdy tree nearby. The mouth of the well gaped open like a dark maw, and as we lowered ourselves into its depths, the world above seemed to vanish, replaced by an overwhelming silence.

The descent was slow, the light from above growing fainter with each passing second. The walls of the well were damp and rough, covered in moss and ancient carvings that seemed to watch us as we passed. Every now and then, I thought I heard whispers, but I dismissed them as tricks of the mind.

When we finally touched down, the ground beneath our feet was uneven and slick. I flicked on my flashlight, its beam cutting through the darkness. The air was thick, heavy with the scent of earth and something else—something old and powerful.

"Look at this," Ben whispered, pointing his flashlight at a series of symbols etched into the walls. "These aren't just carvings. They're part of the seal."

I crouched down, examining them closely. "Elijah must have used these in the ritual. They're worn, but they still hold some power."

We moved deeper into the well's chamber, the air growing colder with each step. The passage was narrow, and the walls seemed to close in around us. It wasn't long before we reached a large stone door, its surface covered in even more intricate runes.

"This must be it," I said, my voice barely above a whisper. "The source of the seal's power is behind this door."

Ben stepped forward, his hand hovering over the door. "But how do we open it? Elijah's journal didn't say anything about a key or a way to unlock it."

I thought back to the ritual, to the symbols and phrases that had been repeated over and over. "Maybe the door responds to the same magic that sealed it. If we can recreate part of the ritual, it might open."

We positioned ourselves on either side of the door, each of us tracing the runes with our fingers. The ancient words felt foreign on my tongue as I began to chant, but they carried a weight, a resonance that seemed to awaken something in the chamber.

The runes began to glow faintly, the light growing stronger with each passing moment. The air around us vibrated, filled with an energy that made the hairs on the back of my neck stand on end.

Suddenly, the door shuddered, the ancient mechanism groaning in protest as it slowly began to open. A blast of cold air hit us, carrying with it the unmistakable scent of something ancient and long-forgotten.

Beyond the door lay a vast cavern, the walls lined with more runes that pulsed with a dim light. In the center of the room stood a pedestal, and on it rested a stone artifact, shaped like a small, intricately carved box.

Ben and I exchanged a glance, our breaths shallow as we stepped into the chamber. The air was thick with power, the very essence of the seal radiating from the artifact.

"This is it," Ben said, his voice reverent. "This is what Elijah used to anchor the seal."

I nodded, my eyes locked on the artifact. "We need to understand how it works. If we can harness its power, we might be able to restore the seal completely."

As we approached the pedestal, a sudden chill ran down my spine, and the whispers that had haunted us since the beginning grew louder, more insistent. Whatever lay beyond the well knew we were here, and it wasn't going to let us leave without a fight

TWELVE

The Heart of the Seal

The cavern was alive with a low hum, a vibration that seemed to pulse through the stone walls and into our very bones. It was as though the very earth around us was breathing, exhaling a slow, rhythmic sigh. The glow of the runes illuminated the chamber in an eerie, dim light, casting long shadows that seemed to move just out of the corner of my vision.

I took a cautious step forward, my flashlight trembling slightly in my hand. Ben was beside me, his eyes wide, scanning the room for anything that might be hiding in the shadows. The pedestal in the center of the cavern, with its stone box, was the only thing that seemed real in this strange, otherworldly place. It beckoned us, as if promising answers—and possibly more danger.

I reached out a hand, my fingers brushing against the surface of the pedestal. The stone was cold, colder than anything I had ever touched, and the moment I made contact, a sudden rush of energy surged through me. It was like electricity, sharp and powerful, but also ancient, as though the very essence of the seal had woken up at my touch.

"Do you feel that?" I whispered to Ben, my voice barely audible over the hum.

Ben nodded, his jaw clenched. "Yeah. It's like the whole place is... alive."

I swallowed hard, my heart pounding in my chest. "This is the source of the seal's power. It has to be."

We both stared at the stone box, its carvings intricate and cryptic. The symbols were familiar now, from the journal and the well, but they were different here—alive, almost. There was a pulsing rhythm to them, as if the artifact was waiting for something.

"How do we unlock it?" Ben asked, his voice strained.

I stepped closer to the pedestal, my hand hovering above the stone box. "I think we need to perform part of the ritual again. We have to activate the artifact. It's the only way."

"But we don't know if that'll work," Ben pointed out, his voice tight with uncertainty. "What if we make things worse?"

I hesitated. It was a valid concern. If the ritual had been broken before, if the guardians had failed, how could we possibly fix it? But we didn't have a choice. The whispers were louder now, echoing in the cavern like a warning we couldn't ignore.

"I know it's risky," I said, meeting his eyes. "But we don't have time to figure out all the answers. The well is weakening, the town is at risk. We have to try."

Ben didn't argue. Instead, he nodded, stepping back slightly as I moved forward. I raised my hands over the box, closing my eyes for a moment as I focused on the words from Elijah's journal, the incantations that had been so difficult to understand. The symbols began to flash in my mind, aligning with the hum in the air. I whispered the first words, my voice shaky but growing steadier as the power from the artifact seemed to respond.

The ground beneath us trembled. A low, rumbling sound filled the cavern, and the air grew thick with an almost palpable force. I felt it in my chest, a pressure that pushed against me, trying to force me back. But I stood my ground, continuing the incantation, the words coming more easily now, as if the artifact itself was guiding me.

Ben took a deep breath and joined me, his voice steady and unwavering as he added his own words to the ritual. Together, our voices echoed through the cavern, the energy around us building to a crescendo.

Suddenly, the stone box began to glow, the runes on its surface lighting up one by one, as if responding to our voices. The hum grew louder, the vibrations in the stone stronger. The pedestal trembled, and for a moment, I thought it might collapse under the force of the power we were awakening.

And then, with a sound like a thunderclap, the box cracked open.

Inside, instead of the ancient relic we had expected, was a swirling mass of shadowy energy, dark and shifting like smoke. It writhed and pulsed with a life of its own, its tendrils reaching out like dark fingers, seeking something. I stumbled back, my heart racing in my chest.

"This... this isn't what I expected," I gasped, fear rising in my throat. "This isn't the source of the seal. It's something else."

Ben's voice was tight with shock. "It's the thing that was locked away. The thing behind the seal."

The mass of darkness inside the box seemed to recognize us, and with a rush of energy, it shot out toward us, faster than we could react. I felt it grab hold of me, a cold, biting sensation that spread from my fingertips up my arm, freezing me to the spot.

I tried to scream, but no sound came out.

Ben lunged for me, grabbing my arm and pulling me away from the tendrils of shadow. His grip was firm, but the darkness didn't relent—it was everywhere, pressing in on us, suffocating us.

"We need to stop it!" Ben shouted, his face pale with fear. "We need to close the box!"

I nodded, my breath coming in shallow gasps. "The ritual—whatever we did, we need to reverse it!"

The shadows writhed around us, trying to drag us toward the pedestal, but we fought back, struggling to break free from its grasp. With every second, it felt as if the darkness was getting stronger, feeding on the energy we had just unleashed.

I looked back at the pedestal. The runes were still glowing, but they were dimming. The seal was weakening again, and the shadows were taking over.

"Ben!" I cried. "We have to reverse the ritual!"

He turned, his eyes wide with panic, but there was no time to think. I forced myself to focus, pushing past the panic and fear, and began to recite the words of the ritual again—this time in reverse.

Slowly, the shadows seemed to pull back, recoiling like something wounded. The air shifted, and the humming sound from earlier grew weaker. The box, too, began to glow again, but this time it was brighter, clearer, as if the seal was being reinforced.

The ground trembled once more, and then, with a final burst of energy, the darkness vanished. The cavern fell silent, the oppressive weight lifting from the air as if the very earth itself was exhaling a sigh of relief.

I collapsed to my knees, gasping for air, my body trembling with the aftermath of the battle. Ben stood beside me, his face pale, his body covered in sweat.

"It's over," he said, his voice low and shaken. "For now."

I nodded, too exhausted to say anything. We had done it. The well was sealed again, but at what cost?

The darkness had been contained, but I knew it wasn't gone. Whatever force we had encountered would be waiting. And the well—Hollowbrook itself—was still at risk.

We had won a battle, but the war was far from over.

THIRTEEN

The Unravelling Truth

The world outside the cavern felt oddly distant, as though the air had thickened, and time itself had warped around us. We had sealed the artifact—at least, that's what we thought. But there was a gnawing feeling in the pit of my stomach, a feeling that told me the battle we had fought beneath Hollowbrook was only the beginning. It had felt like a victory, but deep down, I knew the town was still in peril.

I had hoped, in some small corner of my mind, that once the box had been closed, everything would return to normal. But Hollowbrook was far from normal, and the truth was unraveling faster than we could chase it.

We made our way back up the well, our bodies sore and weary from the ordeal. The air above ground was thick with the same fog we'd encountered before, but there was a sense of foreboding that hung heavier in the mist now, as if it too had felt the shift beneath the earth.

Once we emerged, Ben paused at the top, his face set in a grim expression. “You feel that?” he asked, his voice strained.

I nodded. “Yeah. It’s like the whole town is... different.”

It was hard to put into words, but Hollowbrook felt wrong. The silence was too heavy, and the mist seemed to crawl through the streets like a living thing, wrapping itself around everything. Even the trees, once familiar and comforting, now appeared twisted, as if they, too, were caught in something ancient and dark.

"Do you think it worked?" Ben asked, his voice barely above a whisper.

I wanted to believe that it had—that we had stopped whatever force was threatening the town—but the uncertainty in Ben’s voice mirrored my own doubts. "I don’t know," I said, shaking my head. "But it should have. We sealed it. We reversed the ritual."

But as we made our way back to the town, I realized something was off. The streets were too quiet. The houses stood empty, their windows dark and still. There was no movement, no sign of life. Hollowbrook was eerily abandoned, its people gone without a trace, just as it had been the night before.

"This doesn’t make sense," I said, my voice thick with disbelief. "Where is everyone?"

Ben’s eyes scanned the empty streets, his brow furrowing. "We’ve been down there for hours. But even so... this isn’t normal. People don’t just disappear."

We reached the town square, where the fountain stood still, its water frozen in place as if time itself had stopped. The wind whispered through the trees, but there was no other sound. The entire town seemed suspended in an eerie silence, as if holding its breath.

I walked toward the fountain, my footsteps echoing in the empty square. There was something deeply unsettling about the stillness around us. Hollowbrook had always been quiet, but this was different. It felt wrong, as though something was missing.

"Where is everyone?" I repeated, more to myself than to Ben. "They can't just vanish."

"Maybe they're hiding," Ben suggested, but there was no conviction in his voice. "Maybe they're waiting for us to fix it."

I shook my head. "It's more than that. It's as if... they were never here."

My stomach twisted with an awful realization. The people of Hollowbrook weren't just gone. They had never been here at all. The town itself, the buildings, the streets—they were all wrong. I could feel it now, deep in my bones. The town had never been as it seemed. There was something far darker beneath its surface, something that we had only just begun to uncover.

Ben seemed to sense it too. He turned to face me, his eyes wide with understanding. "It's not just the people. The town itself... it's part of the seal."

I froze, the words echoing in my mind. "What do you mean?"

He gestured to the empty streets, the abandoned buildings. "Everything. The way the town feels... how it's all so perfect but empty. It's like Hollowbrook was built to hold something—a secret—and the moment we started interfering with the seal, it began to unravel."

I looked around again, taking in the quiet streets, the frozen fountain, the dark windows of the homes. The truth was becoming clearer, and with it came an overwhelming sense of dread.

"We thought we were saving the town," I murmured. "But maybe we've been a part of this all along."

Ben's face paled. "What if... what if the town itself was never real? What if Hollowbrook was just a cage—an illusion created to trap us? And by breaking the seal, we've unleashed something that was always waiting for us?"

A chill ran through me. The idea was absurd, but as the fog thickened and the silence deepened, I couldn't shake the feeling that we had stepped into something far darker than we could have imagined.

We stood there, both of us frozen in place, as the mist continued to swirl around us. It was as if the town was watching us, waiting for us to make the next move, and I had no idea what that was. Every step we took seemed to push us deeper into a web of mystery and terror that we couldn't escape.

Then, from the corner of my eye, I saw movement.

I spun around, my heart pounding in my chest. But when I looked again, the streets were just as still, just as empty as before.

Ben stepped closer to me, his voice barely above a whisper. "What was that?"

"I don't know," I said, my voice shaking. "But we're not alone."

Something was out there—something that had been hidden, something that had been waiting. And now, as the fog thickened and the town began to feel even more like a forgotten dream, I realized that Hollowbrook wasn't just a town. It was a prison. A prison built to keep something locked away, and we had just unlocked it.

The shadows were beginning to stir, and with them, the truth we had been running from for so long.

FOURTEEN

THE TRUTH REVEALED

The fog continued to roll through the streets of Hollowbrook, thick and suffocating, blurring the lines between reality and nightmare. The silence was unbearable, pressing in on me from all sides. It felt like the town itself was holding its breath, waiting for something—waiting for us to do something. I could feel the weight of it, like we were being watched by eyes that we couldn't see, and it made my skin crawl.

Ben was walking ahead of me now, his steps slow and deliberate, though I could tell from the way his shoulders were hunched that he was just as unnerved as I was. We hadn't spoken much since our realization that Hollowbrook wasn't just a town—it was part of the seal. Part of the very force we had been trying to fight. And now, it was as if the town was closing in around us, as if it had always been alive, just waiting for the right moment to show its true face.

I caught up to him, my heartbeat thundering in my chest as I spoke. "Ben... What if it's true? What if the town is... the prison?"

He didn't answer right away. Instead, he stopped and turned to face me, his expression hard to read. The worry in his eyes was clear, but there was something else too—something darker, something that told me he was thinking about all the same things I was.

"I think you're right," he said quietly. "I don't know how or why, but I think Hollowbrook is... more than just a town. We've been living in a lie, and now that we've started breaking the seal, the truth is coming to the surface."

The weight of his words hung between us, thick and heavy. For a moment, all I could hear was the distant hum of the town—the strange, low sound that seemed to come from everywhere and nowhere. It felt like the town itself was alive, as if it was listening to our every word, waiting for us to uncover more of its secrets.

"We need to figure out what's behind all this," I said, my voice shaking but determined. "There has to be an explanation. We can't just let it... take over."

Ben nodded, his gaze fixed on the empty street ahead. "I don't know where to start, though. Every time we think we understand something, it only gets more complicated."

I glanced around, my eyes darting from one building to the next. Everything was still. The houses were silent, their windows dark. There wasn't a single soul in sight, but it didn't feel empty. It felt wrong. Like something had been erased. As if the people who had lived here had never existed at all.

A sudden movement caught my eye, and I froze. At the end of the street, a figure stood—shrouded in shadow, barely visible in the dim light of the fog. I couldn't make out any details, but the figure was unmistakably human, and it was standing perfectly still, watching us.

"Ben," I whispered urgently, my voice tight with fear. "There's someone—"

Before I could finish, the figure disappeared into the mist, vanishing without a trace.

My heart skipped a beat. "Did you see that?"

Ben turned, his brow furrowing. "Yeah. But where'd they go?"

I shook my head, my breath coming faster now. "I don't know. But I'm not going to just stand here and wait for whatever that was to come back."

We began walking again, more quickly now, but every step felt heavier. The town had become a maze, its streets twisting and shifting around us, as though the buildings themselves were moving. I kept glancing over my shoulder, expecting to see the figure again, but the streets were just as empty as they had been before.

The oppressive feeling was growing stronger with each passing minute, and I couldn't shake the sensation that we were being pulled deeper into something we couldn't control. Something ancient. Something that had been waiting for us to uncover it.

We reached the town square, the frozen fountain still standing as a silent monument to everything we had uncovered. But this time, it wasn't the fountain that caught my attention—it was the building across from it. The town hall.

It was dark, its windows boarded up as though no one had dared enter in years. But there was a flicker of light from behind the boarded-up windows, a faint glow that beckoned us.

"Let's go," I said, more to myself than to Ben, but he didn't hesitate. He followed me toward the building, our footsteps loud against the cobblestones.

We reached the entrance, and I pushed open the heavy doors, my heart racing in my chest. Inside, the air was thick with dust, the furniture covered in white sheets as though the town had simply been abandoned overnight. But in the center of the room, there was a table—a large, wooden table, old and worn—and on it, a map.

I stepped forward cautiously, my hands trembling as I reached for it. The map was old, faded, its edges frayed as though it had been handled countless times. The town was drawn on it, but the layout was different. Distorted. The streets, the buildings—they were arranged in a way that made no sense. And at the center of it all was a large circle—right where the well had been.

Ben leaned over my shoulder, his breath cold against my neck as he scanned the map. "This... this isn't right. It's not the Hollowbrook we know."

I traced the lines with my finger, my mind racing. "No. This is something else. Something... older. This map doesn't just show the town—it shows the seal. The way it's connected to everything."

Ben's eyes widened. "You mean the town is part of the seal itself? But how? How is that even possible?"

I looked back at him, my thoughts tumbling over each other. "I don't know. But this map... it's like a blueprint. A guide to how Hollowbrook was built to trap whatever's been hidden beneath it."

The glow from the map began to intensify, and I pulled my hand back, feeling the sudden heat radiating from it. The air in the room felt charged, as though the map itself was alive, reacting to our presence.

"We've been following the wrong trail," I whispered, my voice a mix of fear and realization. "The well, the artifact, the seal—it was all meant to keep us from seeing this.

Hollowbrook itself is the key."

Ben's gaze fixed on me, his face pale. "You're saying... the town's been a trap the whole time?"

I nodded slowly, my mind racing. "Yes. The town was built to keep something locked away, and we've just started to unravel it. But now... now we've set it free."

The sound of something scraping against the floor echoed from the hallway outside, breaking the tense silence. We both froze.

"That wasn't us," Ben muttered.

Before I could respond, the door slammed shut behind us, the sound reverberating through the room.

And then the shadows in the corners of the room began to stir.

FIFTEEN

The Final Confrontation

The shadows in the town hall stirred with an eerie kind of life, curling and twisting like smoke. The walls, once solid, now felt like they were breathing, their surfaces undulating as if they were part of some living organism. I could almost hear the walls whispering, echoing voices that weren't my own. The feeling was suffocating, like the room was closing in on me.

I glanced at Ben, whose face had gone pale, his eyes wide with a mix of fear and determination. He was gripping a nearby chair for support, his knuckles white from the pressure. I could see the weight of the situation pressing down on him—on both of us. The realization was clear: we had unlocked something we weren't meant to find. And now, the town, the artefact, the very air around us was responding to our actions.

"We need to get out of here," Ben said, his voice tight with panic. "This place... it's not right. It's changing."

I shook my head, trying to steady my breath. "We can't leave. Not now. We have to understand what's happening, or we'll never stop it."

The shadows in the corners of the room were growing darker, more defined, as if something—no, someone—was watching us. My pulse raced as I turned toward the back of the room, where the flickering light from the map had intensified. The air crackled, a charged energy that made the hairs on the back of my neck stand on end.

"Do you see that?" I whispered.

Ben turned, his eyes following my gaze. The light from the map was no longer just a flicker—it was a bright, pulsing glow, as if the map itself had come alive. The entire room seemed to hum with power, and I could feel it in the pit of my stomach, a deep, primal sense that whatever force we had unleashed was rising.

Without warning, the door to the hall slammed open, and a figure stepped into the room. The mist from outside spilled in with them, wrapping around the figure's form like a shroud. The person was cloaked, their features obscured by the darkness, but I could feel the weight of their presence, pressing against me like a storm.

I stepped back, my heart hammering. "Who are you?"

The figure didn't answer right away. Instead, they stepped into the light, revealing a face I didn't recognize, though something about it felt disturbingly familiar. The eyes were dark, almost black, with no hint of warmth or humanity in them. It was like staring into the abyss.

"Why are you doing this?" I demanded, my voice trembling but firm. "What is this place?"

The figure's lips curled into a cold smile, but their voice was steady, almost soothing. "You've already done it," they said, their voice like a whisper on the wind. "The seal has been broken. The town is mine now."

I felt a cold wave of dread wash over me. "No," I whispered, my voice breaking. "We didn't mean to..."

The figure tilted their head slightly, their eyes narrowing. "Of course you didn't. But you were always meant to. The town wasn't built to trap me. It was built to lure you."

Ben took a step forward, his voice hoarse. "Who are you? What do you want?"

The figure's smile widened, but it was devoid of any warmth. "I've waited for a long time," they said, their voice low and dangerous. "And now, you've released me. Hollowbrook was never meant to be a sanctuary—it was a cage. A cage for something ancient, something older than time itself. A force that cannot be contained, no matter how hard you try."

I took a step back, my mind racing as I tried to piece everything together. The town, the fog, the map—everything pointed to one thing. This person, this... thing, was the source of the darkness that had consumed Hollowbrook. And now, it was free.

"We're not going to let you do this," I said, my voice firm, though my insides were churning. "We're going to stop you."

The figure laughed, a cold, hollow sound that sent chills down my spine. "You think you can stop me? You're already too late. The seal is broken, and Hollowbrook is mine. You cannot undo what has already been set in motion."

Ben stepped up beside me, his fists clenched. "We'll fight you, no matter what it takes."

The figure's expression turned serious, their eyes locking onto mine. "You think you can fight a force like me? I am the darkness that lies beneath your town. I am the fear that has fed on your every hope, every dream. I have waited centuries for this moment."

I didn't know what to do, how to fight something so powerful, so ancient. But I couldn't give up. I couldn't let Hollowbrook—and the people who had been trapped here—fall to this force.

"Ben, the map," I said suddenly, my voice filled with a new sense of urgency. "We need to use the map. It's not just a guide to the town—it's the key."

Ben's eyes widened, and he nodded. "The map... of course. It's the only way we can stop this."

The figure's laughter stopped abruptly, and for a moment, everything was still. The shadows around us seemed to recoil, the air crackling with tension.

"You really think you can undo what's been done?" the figure sneered. "The town is already part of me. The map you hold is useless now. You can't escape what you've unleashed."

But I wasn't listening anymore. I stepped toward the map, my fingers trembling as I traced the lines, searching for something—anything—that might help us. And then, I found it.

A symbol, etched into the center of the map, hidden beneath layers of ink and time. It was a simple design, a circle with an intricate pattern inside it. But as my fingers brushed over it, the air around me seemed to pulse, and a low hum filled the room.

"Ben, help me," I whispered, my heart racing. "It's here. The symbol... it's the key to closing the seal."

Ben rushed to my side, his eyes wide with disbelief. "Are you sure?"

I nodded. "It's the only way."

With trembling hands, I pressed my palm against the symbol, and the room seemed to tremble with power. The shadows recoiled, the figure's form flickering, and I could hear the whispers growing louder, more frantic.

The ground beneath us rumbled as though the very earth itself was shaking with rage. And then, the figure let out a scream—sharp, high-pitched, and filled with fury.

"You cannot stop me!" they screamed, their voice distorting, becoming something inhuman. "I am the darkness that will consume you all!"

But it was too late. As my hand pressed against the symbol, the room exploded with light, blinding and searing. The figure screamed again, a sound of pure agony as the light enveloped them, their form unravelling, dissolving into nothingness.

For a moment, everything went silent.

And then, just as quickly as it had come, the light faded, and the room returned to stillness. The map was gone, and the figure was no more. The oppressive feeling that had hung in the air lifted, and for the first time in what felt like forever, I could breathe.

Ben let out a shaky breath, his hand on my shoulder. "Did we... did we do it?"

I looked around the room, feeling a strange sense of calm settle over me. "I think so."

The shadows were gone, the room now bathed in a soft, warm light that had replaced the cold, oppressive gloom. Hollowbrook was still, but the fear was gone. The town, once cursed and haunted, was free.

But even as I stood there, feeling the weight of everything we had done, I couldn't shake the feeling that this wasn't the end. Hollowbrook had been through so much. And though the darkness had been defeated, I knew the scars it had left would remain.

"We did it," I whispered, barely believing it.

But I knew one thing for sure. Hollowbrook would never be the same. And neither would I.

About The Author:

Author

Ayesha Ashfaque is a 13-year-old writer with a passion for crafting stories filled with mystery, suspense, and adventure. Born with an imagination as vivid as the worlds she creates, Ayesha has been captivated by the power of storytelling from a young age. She enjoys weaving tales that challenge her readers to think, question, and explore beyond the surface, often blending the eerie with the unexpected.

When she's not writing, Ayesha can be found painting, her creativity flowing onto canvases where she explores different artistic styles. She also enjoys reading a variety of genres, drawing inspiration from the books that have fueled her love for fiction. Though this is her debut novel, "The Teen and the Vanishing Town", Ayesha has always dreamed of sharing her stories with the world. Her writing journey has just begun, and she is eager to continue exploring the realms of mystery and intrigue in her future works.

With an unshakable belief that every story has the potential to captivate and inspire, Ayesha hopes her writing will spark the imagination of readers, just as her favorite stories have done for her. She is excited to see where her creativity will take her next and is grateful for the opportunity to connect with readers who share her love for thrilling adventures.

www.ingramcontent.com/pod-product-compliance
Lightning Source LLC
LaVergne TN
LVHW091223150826
845673LV00003B/990

* 9 7 9 8 8 9 6 9 9 2 2 3 3 *